YASMIN
The Fashion Model

written by
SAADIA FARUQI

illustrated by
HATEM ALY

raintree
a Capstone company — publishers for children

To Mariam for inspiring me, and Mubashir for helping me find the right words —S.F.

To my sister, Eman, and her amazing girls, Jana and Kenzi —H.A.

Raintree is an imprint of Capstone Global Library Limited, a company incorporated in England and Wales having its registered office at 264 Banbury Road, Oxford, OX2 7DY – Registered company number: 6695582

www.raintree.co.uk
myorders@raintree.co.uk

Edited by Kristen Mohn
Designed by Aruna Rangarajan
Originated by Capstone Global Library Ltd
Printed and bound in India

ISBN 978 1 4747 6557 2
22 21 20 19 18
10 9 8 7 6 5 4 3 2

British Library Cataloguing in Publication Data
A full catalogue record for this book is available from the British Library.

Acknowledgements
We would like to thank the following for permission to reproduce design elements: Shutterstock: Art and Fashion, rangsan paidaen.

TABLE OF CONTENTS

Chapter 1
A NEW PROJECT 5

Chapter 2
AN ACCIDENT.................................. 12

Chapter 3
ON THE RED CARPET 18

CHAPTER 1

A new project

Yasmin was bored. Really, really bored.

"When will Mama and Baba come home?" she asked her grandparents. "I'm tired of doing crafts. I've already made three bracelets and a crown."

Nani looked up from her sewing. "They've only just left. Be patient. Surely they can have one evening out at a nice restaurant?"

Yasmin scowled. "They promised to bring me pudding. They better not forget!"

She wandered into Mama and Baba's room. Something shiny caught her eye.

Yasmin crept into the huge wardrobe. Brightly coloured clothes were hanging there. Satin kameez, silky hijabs and beaded saris.

It was like a
rainbow swirling
around the room!

CHAPTER 2

An accident

Yasmin couldn't help herself. She had to try on a new kameez she found. She twirled around with arms held out and eyes closed.

"What's going on here?" Nani called out.

Yasmin looked up in surprise.

"Nani, these would look good on you!" She looped a hijab on Nani's head. She wrapped a shawl around her shoulders. "Now we're both fashion models!"

Nani smiled. "I do look nice, don't I?"

The giggles grew louder, and the twirls grew faster, until – OOPS!

Nani stumbled. She stepped on the kameez Yasmin was wearing. Oh no! It was ripped!

Yasmin wailed, "What am I going to do?"

Yasmin took off the kameez. Nani looked at the tear. "Don't worry. I'll tell your mama about it. All will be fine. I can fix it with my sewing machine."

But the fabric was too thick. It broke the needle on the sewing machine.

"I can fix the machine," Nana said. "Just as soon as I find my glasses . . . "

CHAPTER 3

On the red carpet

Nana and Nani were busy fixing the sewing machine. Mama and Baba would be home soon. Yasmin didn't know what to do.

She put on her pyjamas. She tidied up her craft table. Then she had an idea.

"I know how to fix the kameez!" Yasmin shouted. She held up her glue gun.

Nana tried the glue gun and – amazingly – it worked!

Then Yasmin had another idea. She took some feathers and pom-poms and fabric pieces from her craft box. She cut and trimmed and taped them all onto her pyjamas.

Now it was as pretty and colourful as a peacock's tail. Just like Mama's kameez.

They heard Baba's car outside. "They're here!" Yasmin squealed. "Let's surprise them!"

When Mama and Baba came in, the room was quiet and dark. Then Nana flicked a switch. Lights! Music!

"Welcome to Yasmin's fashion show!" he boomed. "Please prepare for our fashion models to wow you!"

Yasmin entered and struck a pose. Her pyjamas shimmered. Her bangles tinkled. Then Nani joined her, modelling a colourful hijab.

Yasmin and Nani paraded up and down the carpet, making sure they didn't fall. Nani waved like the Queen.

Mama clapped her hands to the music. Nana took photos. Baba yelled, "Amazing! Amazing!"

Yasmin smiled and bowed. Then she fell onto the sofa between Mama and Baba. "Phew! I'm starving!" she said. "Did you bring me some pudding?"

Think about it, talk about it

- Yasmin plays dressing up with her nani. What games or activities do you like to do with your relatives?

- Yasmin and Nani accidentally rip Mama's kameez. They fix it and plan to tell Mama when she gets home. Think about what you would do if that happened to you.

- Everyone feels bored sometimes. Make a list of five things you can try next time you feel like there's nothing to do!

Learn Urdu with Yasmin!

Yasmin's family speaks both English and Urdu. Urdu is a language from Pakistan. You may already know some Urdu words!

baba father

hijab scarf covering the hair

jaan life; a sweet nickname for a loved one

kameez long tunic or shirt

mama mother

naan flatbread baked in the oven

nana grandfather on mother's side

nani grandmother on mother's side

salaam hello

sari dress worn by women in South Asia

About the author

Saadia Faruqi is a Pakistani American writer, interfaith activist and cultural sensitivity trainer previously profiled in *O Magazine*. She is author of the adult short-story collection, *Brick Walls: Tales of Hope & Courage from Pakistan*. Her essays have been published in *Huffington Post, Upworthy* and *NBC Asian America*. She lives in Texas, USA, with her husband and children.

About the illustrator

Hatem Aly is an Egyptian-born illustrator whose work has been featured in several publications worldwide. He currently lives in New Brunswick, Canada, with his wife, son and more pets than people. When he is not dipping cookies in a cup of tea or staring at blank pieces of paper, he is usually drawing books. One of the books he illustrated is *The Inquisitor's Tale* by Adam Gidwitz, which won a Newbery Honor and other awards, despite Hatem's drawings of a farting dragon, a two-headed cat and stinky cheese.

Join Yasmin on all her adventures!

Discover more at

www.raintree.co.uk